GRANDPA COMES TO STAY

Rob Lewis

RED FOX

A Red Fox Book

Published by Random House Children's Books
20 Vauxhall Bridge Road, London SW1V 2SA

A division of Random House UK Ltd
London Melbourne Sydney Auckland
Johannesburg and agencies throughout the world

1 3 5 7 9 10 8 6 4 2

First published simultaneously in hardback and paperback by
The Bodley Head Children's Books and Red Fox 1996

Printed and bound in Hong Kong

RANDOM HOUSE UK Limited Reg. No. 954009

ISBN 0 09 933681 2

PEACE AND QUIET
FOR GRANDPA

'Finley! Don't put your feet on the sofa!' said Mum.

'Pardon?' said Finley.

'TURN THE TELEVISION DOWN!' shouted Mum.

'Now, don't put your feet on the sofa.'

'Sorry, Mum,' said Finley.

Finley went into the kitchen. He poured himself a drink of milk and cut some cake. Then he watched television again.

'There are cake crumbs everywhere!' said Mum.

'And you have spilt milk on the table!'

'Sorry, Mum,' said Finley.

'Now listen carefully,' said Mum.

'Grandpa is coming to stay.

He has been ill, he needs peace and quiet.

Noise and mess are not good for him.'

'You mean no loud television?' said
Finley.

'Exactly,' said Mum.

'No feet on the sofa?' said Finley.

'Absolutely not,' said Mum.

'No crumbs?' said Finley.

'Not one,' said Mum.

'No spilt drinks?' said Finley.

'Not a drop,' said Mum.

Grandpa came the next afternoon.

Mum made some tea in the kitchen.

Grandpa turned on the television.

'There's a good match on,' he said to Finley.

Grandpa turned the television up VERY LOUD.

'Goal!' he shouted, jumping up and down on the sofa.

'Finley! Turn off that television!' Mum yelled from the kitchen.

'Grandpa doesn't want a lot of noisy football. I hope you haven't got your feet on the sofa.'

'No, Mum,' said Finley.

'Sorry, Finley,' said Grandpa.

Mum brought in the tea and cakes. Then she took Grandpa's cases upstairs. Grandpa was a bit bored.

'Watch this, Finley,' he said. 'I can balance my cake on the edge of my cup.'

Flop! The cake fell in Grandpa's tea.

'Whoops,' he said.

Mum came downstairs.

'Finley. I told you not to spill any drinks or drop crumbs!

'Grandpa doesn't want a lot of mess around when he's been ill,' she said.

Mum went to get a cloth.

'I only had a cold,' said Grandpa.

'Sorry, Finley.'

In the evening Mum and Dad went to a party.

'Are you sure you're well enough to babysit?' said Mum.

'Yes,' said Grandpa.

Grandpa looked at Finley.

'Tonight,' he said, 'we will put our feet on the sofa.

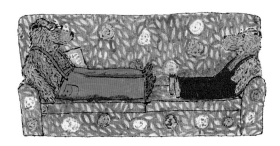

We will turn the television up loud.

We will drop crumbs everywhere and we will spill drinks on the table.'

And they did.

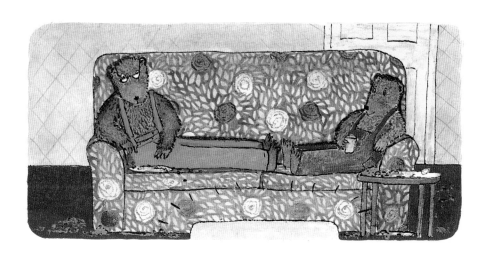

But they cleared up the mess before Mum
and Dad got home.

FISH TALE

Finley and Grandpa went fishing.

They climbed the hill.

'Hurry up Grandpa,' called Finley.

Finley ran down the other side of the hill.

They crossed the river on stepping stones.

'Careful Grandpa,' said Finley. 'You might fall in.'

They sat down on the river bank under a shady tree.

'Shall I put the bait on the hook?' asked
Finley.

'If you like,' said Grandpa.

'Being old can't be much fun,' said Finley.

'Why ever do you think that?'
asked Grandpa.

'You get slow and shaky don't you?' said Finley. 'It must be hard to catch fish.'

'In that case,' said Grandpa, 'how about a competition? *You* fish here and I will fish up river a little way. We will see who has the most fish by lunchtime.'

Grandpa took his fishing bag and his rod and wandered along the river bank until he was just out of sight. Finley started to fish. There weren't many fish in the river. By lunchtime, all he had caught was a couple of tiddlers.

Finley went to find Grandpa. He followed
the path along the river bank but there
was no sign of Grandpa anywhere.

'Maybe Grandpa has got lost?' Finley said
to himself.

Then he saw Grandpa's hat and rod lying
on the path.

'Oh no!' Finley wailed. 'Grandpa has
fallen in the river.'

Finley wondered what to do. 'Why didn't
I look after him properly,' he cried.
Just then, Grandpa strolled along the
path.

'Where have you been?' said Finley, crossly.

'I found a good place to get fish,' smiled Grandpa.

Grandpa showed Finley his bag. The bag was full of fish. They were not tiddlers like Finley's fish. They were big and shiny. Finley was amazed.

'How did you catch those?' he said.

'It takes many years of skill,' said
Grandpa. 'You need to learn where to fish
and how to fish properly.'

'You are clever, Grandpa,' said Finley.

'Will you teach me how to fish properly?'

'Maybe,' said Grandpa.

Grandpa noticed the fish-shop bag
sticking out of his pocket.

He quickly stuffed it back in again.

'Let's build a fire and cook these fish for dinner,' he said.

GRANDPA COOKS TEA

Mum came home from work.

'I'm too tired to cook,' she said.

'Let's have a takeaway,' said Dad.

'It's OK,' said Grandpa. 'I will cook.'

'Are you sure?' said Mum.

'Of course he's sure,' said Finley.

'In that case, thank you,' said Mum.
'There are eggs in the fridge for an
omelette. Finley can help.'

Finley and Grandpa went into the kitchen.

'What flavour omelette are we going to make?' asked Finley.

'Just fetch me the frying pan,' said Grandpa.

Grandpa put the frying pan on the stove. He heated some oil in the pan.

'Eight eggs please,' he said. 'And some milk.'

Finley fetched the eggs and milk from the fridge.

Grandpa put the eggs and milk in the pan.

'But Grandpa!' said Finley. 'You don't put the egg shells in as well!'

'I do,' said Grandpa.

'It's going to be crunchy mushroom and cheese omelette.'

Grandpa added the mushrooms and cheese. He tasted the omelette.

'Hmm… It's not spicy enough,' he said. 'Fetch the mustard, Finley.'

Grandpa emptied the jar of mustard onto the omelette. (He tasted it again.)

'Hmmm… It's not sweet enough,' he said.

'Fetch the marmalade.'

Grandpa emptied the jar of marmalade onto the omelette.

'Hmmm… Not enough filling,' said Grandpa. 'Fetch me a bag of chips from the freezer.'

Grandpa emptied the chips onto the omelette.

'Aren't you going to cook them first?' asked Finley.

'Remember, it's a crunchy omelette,' said Grandpa. 'Chips are crunchier frozen.'

Grandpa tasted the omelette again.

'Hmmm… Not sharp enough,' he said.

'Bring me some lemons.'

Grandpa sliced the lemons onto the
omelette.

'Hmmm… Not chewy enough,' he said.

'Bring me the bag of muesli.'

Grandpa emptied the bag of muesli onto
the omelette.

'Hmmm… Not creamy enough,' said Grandpa. 'Find me two tins of custard.' He emptied the tins onto the omelette.

'Hmmm… Not colourful enough,' said Grandpa. 'Find me the tomato ketchup and a packet of purple jelly.'

Grandpa emptied the ketchup and jelly cubes onto the omelette.

'But Grandpa!' said Finley. 'There's no more room in the pan!'

'That means thc omelette is ready,' said Grandpa.

Grandpa put the omelette onto the plates.

'Only a little bit for me,' said Finley.

Everyone tasted the omelette.

'Quite spicy,' said Dad.

'Quite chewy,' said Mum.

'Quite sharp,' said Finley.

'Lovely and sweet and colourful and
crunchy and creamy!' said Grandpa.

'We're not hungry,' said Dad and Finley.

'I'm too tired to eat,' said Mum.

'In that case, I'll have it all,' said Grandpa.

He emptied their plates onto his plate.

Mum and Dad gave Finley a look.

'Tomorrow we'll have a takeaway,'
they said.